HOW WISE IS AN OWL?

A Question of Science Book

HOW WISE IS AN OWL?

The strange things people say about animals in the woods

by Deborah Dennard
illustrated by Michelle Neavill

 Carolrhoda Books, Inc. / Minneapolis

Each word that appears in **BOLD** in the text is explained in the glossary on page 32.

All photographs by Deborah Dennard except as noted: Merlin D. Tuttle, Bat Conservation International, pp. 23, 24, 25; © Betty Groskin, APSA, p. 27; © Lynn M. Stone, p. 31.

LIBRARY OF CONGRESS CATALOGING-IN-PUBLICATION DATA

Dennard, Deborah.
How wise is an owl? : the strange things people say about animals in the woods / by Deborah Dennard ; illustrated by Michelle Neavill.
p. cm. – (A Question of science book)
Summary: Questions and answers examine and explain common misconceptions about various animals.
ISBN 0-87614-721-X (lib. bdg.)
1. Animals–Miscellanea–Juvenile literature. [1. Animals–Miscellanea. 2. Questions and answers.] I. Neavill, Michelle, ill. II. Title. III. Series.
QL49.D427 1993
591–dc20 92-10354
CIP
AC

Manufactured in the United States of America

1 2 3 4 5 6 98 97 96 95 94 93

For Cleve and Kitty—*D.D.*
For Keith and Kyle—*M.N.*

So, just how wise is an owl?
How blind is a bat?

And how slimy is a snake?

You may think you know the answers, but the truth isn't always what you might expect. People have some odd ideas about the way animals in the woods look, act, and live. Not all of these ideas are true.

Let's take a look at some of the things people believe about animals.

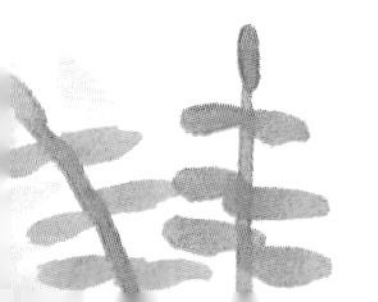

Some people say that wise old owls are as smart as people.

Do you think so too?

Owls are smart at flying and hunting in the dark. At night, they hear the tiniest squeak of a mouse and see the smallest movement of a snake. They know how to find their food and home in a forest. But they can't read a book or teach a lesson! Owls are wise at owl things, not at people things.

Is it true owls can turn their heads all the way around in a circle?

If the bones and muscles in an owl's neck turned too far, they would break.

Look over your shoulder to the right and to the left. You can see all the way around to the back. Owls can do the same thing, only better. They move their heads more smoothly and a little farther, that's all.

There is a reason why owls can turn their heads so well. Hold your head still and move just your eyes to look left and right. Owls can't move their eyes the way you can. To see around, owls must move their heads.

Some people think that snakes are wet and slimy. Do you agree?

Snakes have dry, smooth, and cool skin. Snakes aren't sticky. They aren't slimy or damp or wet. Their shiny skin may look wet, but it isn't. A plastic purse or shoe feels a lot like the skin of a snake.

Do snakes stick out their tongues in warning?

Snakes stick out their tongues, but they're not trying to make you go away. They are tasting and smelling the air!

Snakes investigate the world with their tongues. They find their way and their food through their tongues.

Lizards do the same thing.

Is it true that any snake that bites is poisonous?

Any animal with a mouth can bite! Snakes usually only bite animals that seem like good food. Very few snakes are dangerous to people. In fact, people are more likely to be hit by lightning than bitten by a snake.

How can you avoid poisonous snakes?
Most snakes are harmless. But to be safe, simply do two things. Leave any snake you see alone. And watch where you put your hands and feet when you walk in the woods.
There are three groups of venomous snakes in North America. These are coral snakes, copperheads and water moccasins, and rattlesnakes. These snakes usually stay away from people. They have venom in their fangs to help them get food, not to harm people.

Most snakes squeeze their dinner, then bite it. Some snakes have **venom** in long hollow teeth called **fangs.** When these snakes bite, they force the venom in their fangs into their **prey.** Venom keeps the snake's dinner from running away.

Can you tell a rattlesnake's age by counting its rattles?

Every time a rattlesnake sheds its old skin, it grows a new rattle. Snakes shed their skins as they grow larger.

How? They rub against a rock and back out of the old skin, from tail to head. Snakes pull off the old skin inside-out, just as you might pull off a sock. A well-fed rattlesnake may grow many rattles every year. A hungry rattlesnake may not grow any at all.

Some people think that bats are blind. Do you think so too?

Bats that eat insects usually have small eyes and large ears. Their ears help them move in the dark and find food. As they fly and chase insects, these bats make sounds people can't hear. The sounds move through the air, hit the insect, and bounce back into the bat's ears, telling it just where to look for its dinner. When bats send and receive information through sound, they are using a kind of natural **sonar.**

Will bats fly into your hair?

When bats fly, they sometimes seem to be flying out of control. But they know where they're going. Bats are only interested in hunting insects or finding fruit. They know they won't find food in your hair. And they are such good fliers, they won't end up there by mistake either!

Insect-eating bats can't see very well, but they aren't blind. Their big ears help them "see" in the dark better than most people can.

Not all bats see with their ears. Many bats eat fruit and flowers. They have small ears, but large eyes and noses. These bats use their eyes and noses to see and smell ripe fruit and blooming flowers in the dark.

Some people say that porcupines throw their quills. Do you think so too?

Porcupine quills are stiff hairs used for protection. Frightened porcupines sometimes back into whatever, or whoever, scared them. When they do, their quills make contact and stick. Ouch! Quills do a good job of protecting porcupines from their enemies. But porcupines can't throw their quills.

Can turtles climb out of their shells?

A turtle's shell is made of pieces of bone growing from the turtle's backbone. As a turtle grows, its shell and backbone grow together. You can't have one without the other. A turtle couldn't live without its shell or its backbone.

What animal can climb out of its shell?

Hermit crabs can! Hermit crabs have shells that don't grow from bone in their bodies. Instead their shells are borrowed. Often hermit crabs use empty shells left over from snails. The crabs climb partway into an empty shell and hold on with two legs. Then they walk with their six other legs! When a crab grows too big for one shell, it finds another. But you won't find hermit crabs in the woods. You'll find them at the beach or in a zoo. Some people even keep hermit crabs at home as pets.

So, how much wood can a woodchuck chuck?

Are foxes lazy?

And do bears sleep all winter?

If you think you know the answers, remember, animals aren't always as they seem. And the stories you hear about animals are not always right. To find out which are true and which are not, keep asking questions! The answers will surprise you.

Glossary

fang: A snake's hollow tooth, used to squirt venom into another animal. Snakes that are not venomous do not have fangs. Sometimes the word *fang* is used to describe large teeth in other animals. Cats' teeth are often called fangs, but they are not hollow or filled with venom.

prey: Animals that are hunted by other animals. Prey animals usually have ways to help protect themselves from being eaten. Flying insects may be prey for hungry bats. Rats and mice are prey for hungry snakes.

sonar: A way to find things by sending sound that bounces back to the sender. Bats use sonar. Dolphins use sonar in the ocean. People in submarines use sonar machines as well.

venom: A special kind of poison that is forced into an animal to slow it down or kill it. Bees have venom in their stingers. Venomous snakes have venom in their fangs. Some very unusual fish in the ocean even carry venom in their fins!